THE HOUSE YOU PASS ON THE WAY

OTHER BOOKS BY JACQUELINE WOODSON

From the Notebooks of Melanin Sun
I Hadn't Meant to Tell You This
The Dear One
Between Madison and Palmetto
Maizon at Blue Hill
Last Summer with Maizon

THE HOUSE YOU PASS ON THE WAY

JACQUELINE WOODSON

DELACORTE PRESS

Published by
Delacorte Press
Bantam Doubleday Dell Publishing Group, Inc.
1540 Broadway
New York, New York 10036

The trademark Delacorte Press® is registered in the U.S. Patent and
Trademark Office and in other countries.
"Desperado" by Don Henley & Glenn Frey © 1973 Cass County
Music/Red Cloud Music. All rights reserved. Used by permission.

Library of Congress Cataloging-in-Publication Data

Woodson, Jacqueline.
 The house you pass on the way / Jacqueline Woodson.
  p.   cm.
 Summary: When fourteen-year-old Staggerlee, the daughter of a
racially mixed marriage, spends a summer with her cousin Trout,
she finds herself attracted to Trout and catches a glimpse of her
possible future self.
  ISBN 0-385-32189-9
 [1. Cousins—Fiction. 2. Racially mixed people—Fiction. 3. Interracial marriage—Fiction. 4. Afro-Americans—Fiction. 5. Lesbians—
Fiction. 6. Homosexuality—Fiction.] I. Title.
PZ7.W868Ho 1997
[Fic]—dc21   97–1620
                                                          CIP
                                                           AC

The text of this book is set in 11-point Minion.
Book design by Julie E. Baker

Manufactured in the United States of America
October 1997
10 9 8 7 6 5 4 3 2 1
BVG

For Wendy Lamb, Azali, Kali, and Sadie Rain

And freedom? Oh freedom.
Well that's just some people talking.
Your prison is walking through this world all alone.

It was winter that finally made Staggerlee remember. Something about the way the cold grabbed hold of her as she walked along the river, her dog, Creek, galloping behind her, their shadows like ink against the white snow. And in the distance, the house sitting big and silent with all her family's land spread out beyond it. Even the land seemed vast and muted now. Staggerlee turned to look at it—remembering all the corn and collards, all the wheat that had been harvested. The land didn't seem capable now, flat and snow-covered. All spring, men had come, men her father had hired to work the land. And Staggerlee had watched them moving slowly through the fields, plowing and planting, their faces lined and weathered. Then fall had come, and these same men had returned to harvest the corn and wheat that seemed to grow for miles and miles. Then winter—and the men faded into the thick quiet. Even their laughter—the way it carried back to the house from the fields—where was it now?

1

Staggerlee squinted up at the sun. It was weak today. Wintery. Everything about this place had settled into winter. Even the fish had disappeared, moved closer to the bottom of the river. And the meadowlarks and mourning doves. They were gone too. She shivered, wrapped her arms tighter around herself as she walked. In the distance, a horse whinnied. Creek ran ahead of her, skirting the icy edge of the river.

Autumn had been new—a new school, a new baby sister, the choir. But now she had fallen into the routine of it, and the cold and snow had settled in on Sweet Gum. She walked slowly along the river, picking up shards of ice that had formed along the bank and gazing into them where rainbows shot through in every direction. She stopped walking and turned slowly, full face toward the river. Where would it take her? she wondered. She wished the river were time itself and could take her back to someplace before now. Maybe before last summer. Back to the beginning of her own time. And maybe she could start over there.

And the letter from her cousin, Trout, when it finally arrived late in January, its edges smudged and bending. And the way her legs buckled when she got to the part about—about Trout and . . . Yes, that had made her want to remember. She wanted to make sense of it all, of that summer, of what happened with Trout.

Creek turned and ran back toward her, barking. She reached down to pet him.

"Do you remember it, Creek?" she whispered. "If you could tell the story, what would you say?"

The tiny brown patches above the dog's eyes twitched, and Staggerlee smiled. It always made him seem to be thinking.

"What do *you* remember, dog?" But she wasn't looking at Creek any longer, she was looking out at the river and beyond it—to her own beginning. The river wind blew hard and cold around her, whipping her hair up over her face. It was longer now, and the brown-gold ringlets felt wild in the wind. She closed her eyes and smiled. This was her hair. And her mother's. And her father's.

But her name, Staggerlee, that was her own. A name she had given herself a long, long time ago.

She was born Evangeline Ian Canan at Sweet Gum General, the third of five. Fourteen years ago. Pretty baby. In the baby pictures, she is smiling or reaching up to hug someone. Her hair was red then, and straight. And her eyes were blue like her mother's but had changed over time. Now they were brown. Her mother said she didn't cry often as a child. Staggerlee had gone through the pictures over and over. There were photos of Charlie Horse—her older brother— crying as a baby. Now Charlie Horse was eighteen. When he came home from college at Christmas, Staggerlee showed him the pictures and he laughed. He had a sweet laugh, her brother did. And now Staggerlee smiled, remembering how he'd hugged her and said, "You were just the prettiest of us, girl. That's why there're so many smiling pictures of you." Charlie Horse was older now. College had changed him; he seemed more thoughtful. When he was home, he spent long hours at the piano, practicing right through lunch and dinner. He had always been able to go for hours and hours without eating. Now he seemed able to go days.

And there were crying pictures of Dotti, too. Dotti, who was sixteen now. Smart and popular Dotti. In town, boys and men stared at her, their mouths slightly open. Staggerlee watched them. They were dazzled—as much as she hated that word, it was the only one she could find to describe how people reacted to her sister. But Dotti seemed unaware—almost as though she was looking away from it because she didn't want to see it. Maybe it was because of this—of how beautiful she was—that she worked so hard at school. "My brain's going to be here," she once said to Staggerlee, "way after my looks are gone." And Staggerlee had laughed and said, "Not if you lose your mind." Dotti. Born with Daddy's lips and Mama's eyes. In the baby pictures of her, she looked as though her heart was breaking.

There were even crying pictures of Battle, who was two now, and one or two of Hope—the baby, who still cried and cried.

Again and again she had searched through the photo albums. Again and again she saw the pictures of Evangeline Ian—pretty, smiling baby. As she grew older, that smiling baby girl became her own tiny burden. She was the good child—the happy one. The one that never needed, never asked for anything, never caused any trouble.

It was windy along the river, and cold. She knew by the time she got back to the house her nose and cheeks would be red and numb. Mama would be in the kitchen making lunch or nursing the baby. She closed her eyes. Hope had been born beautiful, with Daddy's broad forehead and Mama's delicate hands. Over the months, as her eyes opened and changed, she became even prettier, and often Staggerlee would come downstairs in the morning to find Mama or Daddy snapping picture after picture. Some evenings she sat on the stairs, half hidden by the banister, and watched them coo over the baby. She wasn't jealous—just curious. Had they been like this with her? Would Hope remember it? Would Hope become a good girl the way she had?

Her father had married a white woman. That's how Sweet Gum people talked about it, talked about her mother. Not to their faces, but it got back to them. The whole family did well at hiding the sting of townspeople's words. It was not *what* they whispered that stung. But how they whispered. Yes, Mama was white and that made all of them—Charlie Horse and Dotti and Battle, Hope and Staggerlee— part white. The only mixed-raced family in Sweet Gum, maybe in all of Calmuth County. No, it wasn't *what* people said, for that part was true. But Mama was more than "white." She was Mama, quiet and

5

easygoing. She kept to herself. When she smiled, her whole face brightened, and tiny dimples showed at the edge of her lips. Why was *white* the word that hung on people's lips? At school, when the kids talked about her mama, they whispered the word or said, "Your mama's *white*!" and it sounded loud and ugly, like something was wrong with Mama. And if something was wrong with Mama, then that meant that something was wrong with all of them.

Some evenings they would sit out on the porch laughing and carrying on and her father would say "Staggerlee, why don't you play us a little song?" Those nights, Staggerlee took her harmonica out of her pocket, ran her tongue over her lips, and started playing. If Dotti was home and in a decent mood, she'd sing. She had a pretty voice. Those evenings, they were not black or white or interracial. They were just a family on a porch, laughing and making music. Those nights, Staggerlee wished they could always be that.

And when people asked her what it felt like to be both black and white, she didn't have an answer for them. Most times, she just shrugged and looked away or kicked her hiking boot against the ground and mumbled something like "fine." Her family had never talked about it, the way they hadn't talked about a lot of things.

Lately, she'd been thinking about God, watching old film footage of her grandparents, listening to the hymns they used to sing. They had been in show business, her father's parents. Grandma could sing a blue streak, and her grandfather was right beside her, dancing, his candy-striped cane flying, tap shoes moving so fast they blurred. Some nights, sitting in the dark, watching old film clips of them performing on *The Ed Sullivan Show*, she would imagine them alive, about to finish up a show and come home.

And last Sunday morning, for the first time in her life, Staggerlee rose at dawn, put on a gray-and-blue dress, pulled the thick blue sweater Mama had knitted over her head, and walked the six miles to Sweet Gum Baptist Church. Some people smiled when they saw her, trying to hide their surprise. A few old women came up to her, asking if she was Elijah Canan's girl. Staggerlee nodded, waved hellos, and took a seat close to the door. She was looking for God, not townspeople. Looking for answers, not questions.

Sweet Gum Baptist is a beautiful church—white walls and high, polished oak pews. On the stage, behind the preacher, there is a stained-glass window. And from the stained glass, a brown-gold Jesus looks out at the congregation. Staggerlee stared up at the glass without blinking. *He looks like me,* she caught herself thinking. *Not black, not white, but both and all of it.* She stared at him so long the colors in the glass blurred—the yellow gold of his robe melted up into the brown disappointment in his eyes. From what seemed like a faraway place, Staggerlee could hear the chorus singing "Precious Lord." Softly. Sweetly.

She could hear the preacher climb the pulpit and

clear his throat. But she could not pull her eyes from Jesus. And the words from the preacher's mouth blended into the stained glass, poured from the clear glass tears in Jesus' eyes and slowly made their way to Staggerlee.

"Truly I say to you . . . one of you will betray me."

Staggerlee blinked. The church felt small and hot suddenly. She could feel Trout pressed into her, shoulder to shoulder, her voice whispery and warm. *Feels like everyone in my life has betrayed me, Staggerlee.*

The organ struck a chord; then the choir started humming. The preacher's voice grew loud, more desperate, but Staggerlee didn't hear the words anymore. Couldn't. The church was closing in around her. She felt herself standing and squeezing past people. Then she was outside, taking in huge gulps of ice-cold air. But Trout was still at her shoulder, her voice still hard against Staggerlee's ear. *Feels like everyone in my life has betrayed me. I guess I'm kind of scared you will too.*

Now Staggerlee shivered, remembering that Sunday. That was before the letter. When months and months had passed with no word from Trout. No, she hadn't betrayed Trout. Now she knew that. She had the letter in her pocket to prove it. And she would read it. Again and again. But first she had to go back to the beginning of all this—had to remember the before time. And maybe if she started from that before place, she'd understand this all.

The sun moved slowly over the water. She hugged herself harder. Her hair blew wild and the wind slapped against her face. Like somebody's cold, cold hand.

CHAPTER ONE

Trout had come to Sweet Gum the first time by letter, a letter from Ida Mae addressed to Elijah Canan—Staggerlee's father. It arrived on a rainy Saturday in April, and while her mother read it, Staggerlee stared out at the rain. She had never met Ida Mae—only knew of her from the stories her father told. Her mother read softly, her eyebrows lifted in surprise. It had been twenty years since anyone had heard anything from Daddy's sisters.

> *Dear Elijah,*
>
> *I know it's been a long time and I hope this letter finds you and yours well. Hallique passed this morning. She had been going back and forth with the pneumonia for a time and one morning, she said to me, "Ida Mae, I just want to lay down and rest." Doctors down in Wartlaw say they did all they could do. You know how they don't care much about colored people nohow so I guess their best was*

the best they could do for somebody that
wasn't white. It's a shame all these years pass
and people still act the way they do. Hallique
passed peaceful, though. In her sleep. I figured
you would want to know being that this is the
only sister we got between us. Now it's just
you and me left of Mama and Daddy's chil-
dren and we haven't seen each other's faces in
nigh of twenty years . . .

When her mother got to the part about Hallique
passing, Daddy started crying softly, one hand pressed
over his eyes. Staggerlee watched him. It was not the
first time she had seen her father cry, but the first time
she had seen him cry so openly, sitting at the table with
all of them around him. Some nights, when they
watched old film clips of his parents performing, his
eyes would fill up and in the darkness of the TV screen
light, he looked thinner and sad-faced.

Dotti got up from the table and put her arms
around his shoulders. She whispered something. Staggerlee stared at them, wondering when Dotti had
become grown-up enough to do something like that.
She wondered what her sister had whispered, why it
had made Daddy nod and pat her hand.

There were photo albums and frames filled with
pictures of Hallique, but the pictures were old, from
years and years ago. In them, Hallique was a teenager,
tall and thin like Daddy, with dark suspicious eyes.
Staggerlee stared out at the rain slamming against the
window and imagined it was the spirit of Hallique

11

trying to get inside. Trying to get a good look at them all once, just once, before moving on to the next place.

"Was she good, Daddy?" Staggerlee asked softly.

All spring she had been thinking about good and bad. She didn't understand it—what made a person good, what made a person bad. She didn't know what *she* was. At school, kids said she was stuck-up, thought she was better than other people. Maybe she was stuck-up. Maybe she did think she was better. She didn't know. So she remained quiet, watched people without joining in. Did that make her bad? Seemed all the girls at school knew who they were somehow. The way they dressed. The way they moved in clusters—laughing and holding their books tight to them. The way they sloe-eyed the boys. She knew she didn't want this—to be a hanger-on, a follower, a part of somebody else's pack. But then what was left? Where did she fit in? All her life she'd been thinking it was the mixed blood— the black and the white of her leaving her somewhere in the middle of things. But that wasn't it. Charlie Horse and Dotti moved so freely in the world, and they had the same blood running through their veins. No. It was something deeper—something lonely inside of her. Something quiet.

And the night before—what about that? The night before Ida Mae's letter came, something had happened to Staggerlee. Something hushed and solemn her mother said happened to all girls. And after they had spoken, Mama brought Dotti in to join them and they drank wine from a small crystal glass. A celebration, Mama whispered. But maybe it was bad, this thing that

12

had suddenly changed her from a girl to a woman. Because she couldn't tell the men about it, not her father, not Charlie Horse, who she had told everything to always. Why did she have to start having secrets from him? What was so bad about it?

"Was she good, Daddy?" Staggerlee asked again, pressing her hand against her stomach. All morning long, dull pains had been shooting through it. "Hallique. Was she a good person?"

Her father frowned.

Hallique and Ida Mae had stopped speaking to him when he married Mama. They said they didn't have anything against white people, they just didn't want them in the family. That was twenty years ago. Staggerlee looked down at her arm while she waited for him to answer. Her arm was pale now. By the end of summer, it would be amber.

"Yes," her father said finally. "Underneath all the things Hallique did and said, she was good."

"But she hated us," Dotti said.

Mama shook her head. "She didn't know you. It was the idea of us she disapproved of."

"The *idea* of us." Dotti rolled her eyes. "Well, I can't grieve the *idea* of her passing."

"I would've liked to have known her," Staggerlee said. "Even for just a minute. I would have liked to look in her eyes, her true live eyes, just once before she died. I would have said, 'Hallique, look at me. I'm your niece. Your blood kin.' "

The family sitting around her was the only family she knew. No aunts or uncles or grandparents. No

13

cousins or nephews. Just what was in this kitchen and the baby her mother was four months pregnant with. Staggerlee looked around at everybody. Suddenly they seemed small, like a tiny raggedy army trying to hold on.

Charlie Horse was sitting away from them on a stool at the counter. He sniffed, and Staggerlee wondered if he was trying not to cry. She wanted to hug him the way Dotti was hugging Daddy. A year ago she would have. Even a week ago. But now she felt strange, distant—different from him. When she was young, they would spend hours sitting out by the river. Charlie had played piano since he was two. He would sit by the river with his hands out in front of him as if they were resting on the black and white keys of his piano. And he'd talk about the songs he was going to write one day while his fingers danced excitedly—like they could hardly wait.

"Hallique was the one who sang," Charlie Horse said now, looking down at his fingers. Maybe he was thinking of the music he and Hallique could have made together. "She cut a couple of records, didn't she?"

"Two," Daddy said. "Cut two records back in sixty-eight. But when she and Ida Mae were so mean about your mama, I threw those records out." His eyes filled up again. When they were young, Daddy had told them once, Hallique would dress him up in her frilly blouses and push him around in a stroller with her baby dolls. He said he loved the way she took such time with him, unlike Ida Mae, who was older.

"Somebody should have been strong enough to say something," Charlie Horse said softly. "Twenty years is a long time to go without speaking."

Staggerlee nodded. No one talked about the twenty years of not speaking. It was an unwritten rule.

Battle started whining to get down from the high chair. Staggerlee reached over and pulled him out and watched him take off for a stack of toys in the corner of the kitchen. She excused herself to go to the bathroom.

In the bathroom, she stared into the mirror. She had grown taller over the winter, and her hair had gone from dark to reddish brown. She pulled a lock of it down over her eye and watched it spring back. Her lips were full across her face like Daddy's. What had Hallique known about them? That they were mixed-race, black and white joined together—what their grandparents had fought for and what had killed them.

Staggerlee took a step back from the mirror and pressed her hand against her chest. Her breasts were sore. Her mother had said this would pass. How long? What had it been like for Dotti the first time? And Mama? She hadn't said much to her and Dotti last night. Mama was quiet that way. "I'm used to working things out on my own," she had said once. "In my own mind."

"Ida Mae and Hallique were already living in Maryland when your grandparents died," her father was saying when Staggerlee came back to the kitchen. "I was up in New York. We all came back here for the funeral. Must of been a thousand-something people paying their respects." He sniffed. "I brought your

15

mama. . . . We'd been dating a couple of months by then."

"They know the story, Elijah," Mama said. Daddy ignored her. Mama was wrong. They knew bits and pieces of a hundred stories. But not one whole one.

Mama pulled her needles and yarn from a bag beside her chair and started knitting. The yarn was a soft blue that made Staggerlee think of cornflowers. Once when Staggerlee had asked her mother about learning to knit, her mother had said, "My mother taught me." Something in her mother's voice let Staggerlee know that that was all she was going to say about it. Mama's parents had disappeared a long time ago—they hadn't approved of the marriage either. Some days, Staggerlee felt surrounded by disappeared people, old photographs and bits of stories of people who had long ago left the picture.

"My sisters didn't like the idea of me and Adeen being together," Daddy was saying. "Ida Mae was a big revolutionary back then, and Hallique bonded to Ida Mae after our folks died."

"That was the last we saw of them," Mama added.

Daddy nodded. "I wrote and invited them to the wedding, but they never showed. Didn't even reply to the invite. Wrote again to let them know me and Adeen had moved back here to Sweet Gum and that Adeen was pregnant." He pointed his chin at Charlie Horse. "Called them a couple of times back then, but they'd stopped answering their phone. Heard from some folks that Ida'd married, and I didn't even know her last name anymore."

"What about Hallique?" Dotti asked.

"Couple of years back," Daddy said, "she wrote saying she wanted things to be better between us. Wanted to get to know you all . . . said she was sorry for all those years she didn't speak or write or send a birthday card . . ."

Mama was knitting faster now, her fingers blurring across the yarn.

"You never wrote her back, did you?" Staggerlee bit her bottom lip.

Daddy shook his head, pulled his hand across his eyes.

"What about us?" Staggerlee said, her heart pounding hard against her chest. "What about us, Daddy?"

"Staggerlee." He slammed his hand against the table. "I didn't think she'd die." He started crying again, hard, loud sobs. "I thought there'd be time."

Her mother reached across the table and stroked her head.

"I want to hear the rest of Ida's letter." Staggerlee pulled away from her. "Before someone gets the keen idea to throw it away."

Her mother started reading again, looking at the letter over her knitting.

> ". . . *My husband Jonathan woke up from a nap this afternoon saying he had had himself a dream about you all and all day long, that dream stayed on his mind. He and I got to talking and we figured all these years of having the family all disconnected have just*

17

been a waste of good living. We want to come
visit and have you all come to Maryland—
the whole family. Last I read, you was about
to have a third child. I guess it might just be
more than that by now. Jonathan's teaching
at Old Dominion these days and this summer
we're already too busy to think about a trip
further south. Some time ago, we adopted us
the sweetest baby girl. We call her Tyler after
Mama's sister Tyler—the one that passed a
few years before Mama and Daddy did. Tyler
says she wants to come spend some time with
you all this summer and me and Jonathan sat
and talked and figured it was high time to
start the reuniting process. Tyler'll be fifteen
come fall. I put one of her school pictures in
with this letter. . . ."

"My age?" Staggerlee said. "She's my age?"

Her mother reached inside the envelope. She studied
the picture a moment before handing it around the
table.

Staggerlee stared at the photo. It wasn't a regular
school picture—the head-shot kind with a bookshelf
or an American flag waving behind the person. In the
photo, Tyler was standing in a field. In the distance, a
cheerleading squad was practicing, and even further
out, a football team was running in a straight line. But
right up front, in the middle of the frame, Tyler stood
dressed in black, her hands on her hips, looking side-

long at the camera as if she were daring the photographer to say smile.

"Looks like she has an edge to her," Mama said.

Staggerlee looked at the picture again. Tyler reminded her of Hazel, this friend she had once. She didn't look anything like Hazel, not really, except for the way she was looking at the camera—looking at *Staggerlee*—skeptical, like she'd heard every story in the world a million times.

"I want her to come," Staggerlee said, staring at the picture.

"We'll see how the rest of the spring goes—"

"No 'we'll see,' Mama. I want her to come!"

Mama looked at her sharply, but Staggerlee glared back.

"It's always 'we'll see.' You'd think after twenty years, we'd be jumping at the chance to *see* some family."

"She's adopted, anyway," Dotti said.

"Still family," Staggerlee said. "If Daddy's sister raised her."

Dotti ignored her.

"It's a lot of thinking to do, Stag," Daddy said softly. "We barely know them—never even met Jonathan and Tyler. And with all this stuff going on—"

"I know."

A month before, Mama's doctor had told her she'd have to take time off from her job as a paralegal, and stay off her feet as much as possible if she wanted the baby born healthy. Charlie Horse had pretty much taken over for her, cooking all the family's meals and staying on Staggerlee and Dotti to keep Battle and the house clean.

Mama got up and set the kettle on the stove for tea. She moved slowly, one hand beneath her small stomach.

"It's not about Ida Mae and Hallique," Staggerlee said. "Not anymore anyway. It's about Tyler. That's who I'm asking you to say yes to."

Dotti frowned. "Well, if she comes, don't expect me to be taking care of her, showing her around—"

"Nobody expects anything from you, Dotti. And, boy, do you deliver." Staggerlee glared at her sister, running her tongue over the place where one of her front teeth overlapped the other. Dotti was only two years older, but she was a stranger more than a sister. At sixteen, she was filled with what Mama called "a restless spirit." She had their mother's thick black hair coiling down past her back and straight white teeth like Daddy. And unlike Staggerlee, Dotti was always surrounded by friends. Twice she'd gotten voted most popular, and once, prettiest. The last time Staggerlee had invited her to walk along the river, Dotti had frowned like it was a ridiculous idea. *She doesn't understand the river the way I do,* Staggerlee remembered thinking. *The way you can come across somebody fly-fishing if you get up early enough or close to evening. The sound of the reel is pretty.* Some days, watching the fishermen, she started thinking she really didn't need anybody else. But there were nights when she stood

20

outside Dotti's bedroom door, listening to her and her friends.

Dotti started clearing away the breakfast dishes.

"Are you going to say yes?" Staggerlee turned back to Mama. "You don't have to do anything, Mama. I'll do it. And maybe Tyler could help out too."

Her mother's face softened. She looked at Staggerlee a long time. And Staggerlee felt embarrassed. Was it that obvious, she wondered, how lonely she was? She thought about turning away, hiding her face from Mama. But she didn't. Maybe a year ago she would've ducked her head or blinked. But she was a woman now. Mama had said so.

"If it's that important to you then, honey . . ." She turned to Daddy.

"Then yes—yes, Tyler can come," he said.

Staggerlee smiled, picking up Tyler's picture again. "Yeah," she said. "It's that important."

CHAPTER TWO

She had kissed a girl once. In sixth grade. Hazel. She didn't remember how she and Hazel started being friends. Hazel showed up to school late in the year and somehow they had just started hanging together. Hazel's mother made all her clothes and didn't allow her to wear anything but dresses that stopped right below her knees. All her dresses were pastel—even in the winter, she would show up to school in pale green and blue dresses with huge sashes tied in the back. The dresses made her look young and old at the same time. Her hair was thick and coiling, but her mother made her wear it pulled back into a tight braid. At school, Hazel undid her braid and let her hair go wild. She had a way of laughing that made Staggerlee feel warm and safe. They had kissed after school one day, behind a patch of blue cornflowers.

Soon after, Staggerlee came down with the chicken pox and ended up staying home from school for a week. She didn't mind that Hazel didn't come visit—their house was far away from everyone and hard to get to. When she returned to school, Hazel was huddled in the schoolyard with a group of girls. Staggerlee walked toward them slowly, knowing something terrible was about to happen. They were whispering, but as she got closer they stopped, and Hazel turned slowly, her lavender old-lady dress spinning out from under her.

Staggerlee touched her fingers to her lips, wanting Hazel to remember the way the cornflowers had swayed, the way the sun set down all gold and pretty that afternoon. Wanting her to remember how she had said, "I could stay here forever—just me and you right here in all of this blue." But when Hazel turned to her, her eyes were blank, unfamiliar. A stranger's eyes.

"Your grandparents was killed by a bomb?" she asked, her eyes slitted. "Those Canans they got the statues of up in town—those were your people?"

"Were," Staggerlee said. "Before I was born. They were my grandparents, but I didn't know them." Behind Hazel, the other girls looked on, their lips hard across their faces.

"You never told me that, Stag," she said, her voice all full of hurt. "All these things I'm hearing now that you never told me."

"It's nothing, Hazel. Doesn't have anything to do with me. This is me—the person you see standing here. I didn't even know them."

Someone giggled.

"That's 'cause they died," one of the girls—a girl named Chloe—said. "And they must have left y'all lots of money and everything. That's why you think you better than everybody else, 'cause of your grandpeople. That's why y'all live way out like you do and you think you too cute to talk to anybody."

"I don't think I'm better or cute. Hazel, you know that."

"You didn't tell me. You made believe you were just regular, like all of us. But you ain't."

They stared at each other for a long time. That afternoon, nestled down in the cornflowers, Hazel had put her hand on Staggerlee's cheek and said, "You're beautiful, Staggerlee. Inside and out. I wish I was beautiful inside and out like you." Staggerlee swallowed. She should have told Hazel then that she thought she was beautiful too. All the things she should have said to Hazel came rushing to her at once.

"Plus, she got a white mama, Hazel. I bet she didn't tell you that either," another girl said—a light-skinned girl everyone called Bug because of her small head and big dark eyes.

Staggerlee glared at her. Her father had said African Americans were all mixed up—not just the out-and-out mixed-raced kids, but that all black people weren't a hundred percent African unless they never left Africa. He said most likely even the darkest black had some white blood somewhere in their veins, and the lighter ones, well, unless they were albino Africans, then they had some too.

"And her mama thinks she's better than everyone too—just cause she's white," Bug continued.

"You don't even know my mother," Staggerlee

24

whispered, feeling herself turning to stone. She wanted to disappear, to melt into the ground and be gone.

"Everyone knows your mama. It's only three, four white women in all of Sweet Gum and only one of them married to your daddy. My ma see her in town say she don't hardly speak to people, all these years she been in Sweet Gum. Nobody needs y'all."

"She doesn't speak to people 'cause that's her way," Staggerlee said, hating her mother, how quiet and inside herself she was in public. She had never been like Daddy, who seemed to know everyone in town. He was full of "Good mornings" and "What you know goods," grinning and slapping men on the back, winking and tipping his hat to the women.

"Well, nobody needs 'her way.' "

"Just rude and stuck-up," Chloe said. "Your whole family think they so cute. Bug's right—nobody needs y'all."

Staggerlee swallowed. "How about you, Hazel?"

Hazel glanced away from her. When she looked back, her eyes were cold.

"No," she said, turning back to the group. "I don't need you."

Staggerlee blinked, her eyes burning. But she wasn't going to cry. Not in front of them.

CHAPTER THREE

It rained hard all weekend. Early Sunday morning, Daddy sat down to write Ida Mae a long letter saying they were looking forward to having Tyler at the house and that he hoped this was the beginning of the family coming back together. Staggerlee sat across from him at the kitchen table, playing her harmonica softly, every now and then listening to him read paragraphs out loud to see if they sounded okay.

"Why don't you just call her?"

Her father pressed the pen against his lips. "I can't," he said quietly, looking over at her. "After all these years. I called so much early on." He leaned back over the letter. "And there're other reasons too. They probably still don't answer their phone."

Staggerlee nodded. They had stopped answering their own phone a long time ago, letting the answering machine pick up and screen the calls. Mama had finally gotten tired of the press calling all the time, asking them questions about Daddy's parents. Biographers and film producers were also calling for a while—wondering if they could get the rights to write the book or make the movie of their lives.

"You think Tyler'll come, Daddy?" She looked at him, trying not to seem too hopeful.

"Yeah, she'll come," he said. But he was concentrating on his letter. Staggerlee stared at the top of his head. His hair was thick and nappy. When she was little, she would run her hands through it, laughing, loving how warm and springy it was.

THAT NIGHT, as they sat watching film clips of the grandparents, Staggerlee couldn't get her mind off Tyler—wondering what it'd be like to have her in the house. In the blue-gray light of the television, the family looked strange and beautiful. Charlie Horse was sitting across from her with Battle halfway asleep on his lap. Her parents were on the couch, Daddy's arm around Mama's shoulder. Staggerlee pressed her face into Creek's head. He smelled of grass and river. Dotti was lying on her back, close up on the television, her hair spread out like some curly fan above her head.

"Here comes the part when Papa sings your song, Stag," her father said.

On the screen, their grandfather was doing a slow soft-shoe. When he started singing, his voice was raspy and soft as a whisper.

> *He ain't had no limits, that ole boy, Staggerlee,*
> *Put him in a prison box, he'd find the key or*
> *   break that lock*

Couldn't keep him locked inside, that ole boy,
   Staggerlee.

It had taken Staggerlee years of listening to that song to understand it.

"Everyone said Staggerlee was a bad, bad cat," Daddy said. "But listen to that song. My daddy had a whole different take on him."

On the screen, her grandfather's face broke into the same grin as Daddy's, and Staggerlee watched him, watched him slide across the stage, doing fancy spins, then breaking into a high-stomping tap.

He didn't have no children. Didn't have no wife
Said, "Your Honor, the only thing I got is my
   life. Please don't take that."
He was a slick one, that old boy, Staggerlee.

The legend had it that Staggerlee had shot a man for a five-dollar hat and went on to be known as the most evil man alive. Staggerlee squinted at the television, listening to her grandfather and the story inside the story. It wasn't about murder at all—it was about someone struggling to break out of all the gates life had built up around them. She was nine when the words started making sense. Nine when she changed her name. And although it had taken the family a while to get used to it, they did. Sometimes, when her mother was angry or tired, she slipped back to Evangeline. But Staggerlee wouldn't answer to it. At school she insisted on being called Staggerlee.

Staggerlee went to Heaven but Heaven's gate
  was closed
St. Peter told him, men like you be better off
  down below
Staggerlee went on down there, but the Devil
  turned his back
Staggerlee said, "There ain't no right or wrong.
  There ain't no white or black . . ."

"If they'd only done one more show," Dotti said, turning away from the screen.

It was the last show their grandparents had done before they died. The film clips were grainy—black-and-white images that had that long, long time ago look about them.

Staggerlee's grandparents had been on their way out the door to the demonstration for an all-boy school in Monroeville, Alabama, that refused to integrate when someone from *The Ed Sullivan Show* called.

"The response to the last show had been so over-whelming," her father said to Dotti. Again and again he'd told this story. Staggerlee stared at the TV screen. Maybe she'd heard it a dozen times. Maybe a hundred. If her father told it enough, she wondered, did he think he could change the ending?

"They wanted them to come back to New York to do another show," her father was saying. "Would fly them out that evening and have them home by the next day if they needed to be. But you see, they were already committed to this demonstration. Hallique was living here at home then—going to college nearby in Bakersville. I was already in New York. She sat there listening to them go back and forth about it. Said she was mad. Had a basketball game that night and wanted them to be there. She was playing college ball—one of the first black women on the team. Hallique told me that Mama and Daddy were standing in the kitchen trying to decide between Ed Sullivan and Monroeville and she was sitting at the table dressed in her basketball uniform hoping they'd just forget both things and come watch her play." He got quiet for a moment. When he started speaking again, his voice was softer. Staggerlee leaned back against his legs. He stroked her head as he spoke.

"By this time, they were well known. They knew their appearance at a demonstration meant a lot to the press. And this was supposed to be a big one, with news crews and national papers coming—three gospel choirs from churches as far off as Berkeley, California. Even the Vice President talked about showing."

Her father got quiet again. He always got quiet at this point. It was too hard for him to say—the part about the bombing. Hallique had gone to her game that night and was on her way home when two men ran up and asked if she was Hallique Canan. Staggerlee pressed her cheek against Daddy's knee. Mama had told them this part—about how the men had told Hallique about the bombing, about her parents dying. She had never heard her father say it—say the words— that his parents had died that night.

"Hallique said they won their game that night," her father said softly.

STAGGERLEE SAT WATCHING that same film clip over and over, long after everyone else had gone to bed. Her grandmother's voice rose up sweet and high as she sang "I Wonder as I Wander." Staggerlee sat there wondering if her grandparents had found a home somewhere, a place where there was nothing left to fight against. She watched their grainy faces smiling into the camera and wondered how long they'd all be wandering.

CHAPTER FOUR

News traveled quickly through Sweet Gum. That spring, Staggerlee heard that Hazel was leaving, that her family was moving the first of the month. In school they had hardly spoken. Some mornings, as they passed in the halls, Staggerlee would absently press her fingers to her lips. She wondered, now, as she sat on her porch, if Hazel had forgotten that afternoon in the cornflowers. And if she had, what thoughts, what friendships had replaced the memory? Staggerlee stared out at the sun setting bright orange beyond the fields. Tall stalks of corn swayed slowly, and their shadows, casting out over the land, filled Staggerlee with a sadness she couldn't name. She was waiting for Hazel. Even though they hadn't spoken in a long time, she was hoping Hazel would come by before she moved. To say goodbye. To say that she remembered.

Early in the evening, Staggerlee's father returned from work and sat with her.

"You look like you're waiting for someone," he said, smiling.

Staggerlee shook her head.

"I used to sit like this," Daddy said softly. "After my parents died, I'd just sit on this porch waiting for them to come on home. Ida and Hallique'd be inside and I'd be sitting here. On these stairs."

"But you knew they weren't coming home."

"That didn't stop me from waiting for them. I wasn't much more than a boy. Probably still believed that if you wished hard enough you could make the impossible happen." He took his pipe from his back pocket, put it in his mouth, and struck a match to it. Cherry-scented smoke circled them.

"You never met my friend Hazel," Staggerlee said.

Daddy squinted as though he were thinking. "I never met any of your friends and you know it." He winked at her.

Staggerlee smiled, pulled her knees up to her chest, and wrapped her arms around them. At first her parents had worried about her social life. But a long time ago, she had convinced them that her harmonica and Creek were enough. That she didn't need a roomful of friends, like Dotti.

"Hazel's the only one, really," she said. "I mean she used to be."

"Used to be?"

"She's moving. Her daddy took a job down in Florida. I was thinking she'd come by to say goodbye."

Her father looked thoughtful for a moment. They sat for a while without saying anything.

"Sometimes people don't get a chance to say goodbye, Stag."

He put his arm around her shoulder and pulled her closer to him.

"I'm always gonna take the time," she said. "No matter what happens."

"That's good. Always take the time. You really never know when you're not going to have it anymore." He stuck his pipe back in his mouth and puffed on it. They sat quietly, staring out at the fields. Staggerlee glanced toward the road.

"Charlie Horse got a letter today," she said. "A place for him to study piano opened up at that music camp. He'll be leaving by the end of the week."

"That so," Daddy said, frowning.

Staggerlee nodded. All winter Charlie Horse had been waiting for this letter—a full ride to one of the country's most prestigious music camps. He'd start college straight from there. They probably wouldn't see him again until Thanksgiving. Staggerlee swallowed. First Hazel, now Charlie Horse. Seemed like this town, their house, was all just something you passed on the way.

"Why'd you come back to this house, Daddy?" It was getting dark quickly now, and around them, katydids were starting to call out. Inside, she could hear her mother and Charlie Horse getting dinner ready.

Her father took a long drag on his pipe. "I always knew I'd come back here. This house gets in your blood. I sit on the stairs sometimes and remember Mama on her hands and knees polishing those floors, remember my father outside high up on the ladder laying down shingles. Some mornings I wake up and she's right in that kitchen taking a pan of biscuits from the stove."

He got quiet for a moment.

"They left this world," he said softly. "But they never left this house. I had to come back to them."

"You think Charlie Horse'll come back here?"

"A couple of times probably. The way you and Dotti will after you're gone. I don't expect any of you to settle here the way I needed to."

Staggerlee stared out at the road, knowing, all at once, that Hazel wasn't coming, that they had said their goodbye that morning in the schoolyard over two years ago.

She leaned against Daddy's shoulder in the darkness and listened to the river rush past.

CHAPTER FIVE

School ended on a Thursday at the end of May. All the eighth-graders were headed for Sweet Gum High come September, and the girls dressed up that last day in ankle-length dresses and high heels. *Maybe they're practicing for high school,* Staggerlee thought, sitting at the top of the school stairs watching them, *trying to make themselves feel older, grown-up already.*

Precarious. That was the word that kept coming to mind. The night before, her mother had said it about Battle—that he seemed so precarious when he ran. And now, watching these girls make their way to the school buses and waiting cars, Mama's word for Battle kept popping into her head. They seemed scared too and unsure of themselves behind the thick mascara and painted-on lips.

Staggerlee pulled her sweatshirt away from her chest and blew down into it. It was an old Columbia shirt that had once belonged to her father. He had gone there for two years before dropping out to learn to fly planes. He had a small airport down in Anderson, taking people down to and back from the Sea Islands. Her mother had gone to Mount Holyoke, and more than once she had told them she'd be proud if Staggerlee or Dotti followed in her footsteps. Staggerlee had pulled the sweatshirt on this morning without thinking about how hot she'd be in it. And now, as the sun beat down on her, she pushed the sleeves up past her elbows and squinted into the crowds. She looked so different from everyone. Her clothes, the thick-soled hiking boots, her hair. And she felt different too—off-step somehow, on the outside. What did it sound like, Staggerlee wondered, having someone call your name across a crowded schoolyard? How did it feel to turn to the sound of your name, to see some smiling face or waving hand and know it was for you and you alone?

Staggerlee watched the students piling onto the school buses. She would walk home today—six miles. Maybe she'd run into her mother and Battle along the way, coming from shopping in town. Yes, that would be nice, to steal up behind them and wrap her arms around Mama's waist. To see Mama turn, then smile and hug her. To see Battle laughing with surprise.

The stairs were almost empty. Staggerlee took her harmonica from her pocket and started blowing.

Charlie Horse was gone now. He had hugged her hard the morning he left and promised to write. It hadn't seemed real that day, his leaving. As Staggerlee stood on the porch watching him and Daddy drive off, she waved absently, a part of her believing he'd be back in a day or two. But now it was starting to settle in. The house felt emptier without him. Some mornings, she ran her fingers along the piano wishing he were there playing. When she plucked at the keys, they echoed through the house and faded. It felt as if the house itself were missing Charlie Horse.

When the last school bus drove off, Staggerlee looked around her.

Tyler would arrive next Thursday, and Staggerlee and Daddy would pick her up in Tudor—a small town about fifty miles north of Sweet Gum.

Staggerlee ran her tongue over her harmonica and wondered for maybe the thousandth time what it would be like to have Tyler staying with them.

It was sunny and warm now. All around her, sugar maples and silver birches were beginning to bloom. She blew a note, soft and clear. Was Tyler up in Baltimore, packing slowly and thinking about coming?

CHAPTER SIX

It rained the morning they left for Tudor. Red mud trails flowed down away from the house on the Breaka-bone River side. Staggerlee sat in the truck staring out the window while her father gave last-minute instructions to Dotti.

"How come Staggerlee can't stay home with Battle?"

"I'll stay," Staggerlee lied. "You can go with Daddy to Tudor."

"I don't want to go to nobody's Tudor." Dotti glared at Staggerlee. All morning she had complained about not being the one who wanted Tyler to visit, that it wasn't fair that she was stuck with Battle now that Charlie Horse was gone.

"If Battle wakes up," Daddy said, "give him the juice bottle. There should be some crackers he can chew on in the cabinet."

Dotti stood on the porch looking evil. She was wearing a pair of short-shorts and a near-transparent shirt over a black bra.

"Don't wake Adeen either. No company. No loud music. You hear me?"

"I heard you," Dotti said, rolling her eyes. "I'm going to Jen's when y'all get back."

"Maybe," Daddy said, climbing into the truck. "Maybe when we get back you can change your clothes and go on over to Jen's."

Dotti turned on her heel and slammed inside the house.

"Don't know what we're going to do about her," Daddy said, starting the car and moving slowly down the long driveway. "Girl's becoming hard to live with."

"Ma says it's just her taking being a teenager too seriously. A phase."

"Well, it would be nice if you remembered how troubling this phase is for us and not make us go through it again."

"I'm not Dotti."

"I know." But he looked worried anyway.

Staggerlee stared out the window. Would there ever come a time when her parents weren't comparing her to Dotti or using Dotti's bad behavior to teach her a lesson? Her mother had said that she and Dotti were both women now. *But still,* Staggerlee thought, *I'll never be her.* That was the thing her parents would never understand.

AS THEY NEARED TOWN, Staggerlee's stomach tightened. Town made her nervous. There was always

40

someone somewhere ready to point them out, ready to whisper, "You remember that bombing back in sixty-nine? Well, that's the family of those people." Some days she felt like a sideshow act—being gawked at by people she didn't know.

People were walking fast underneath brightly colored umbrellas. A couple waved, and her father waved back. A group of men sitting underneath a gas station awning grinned and waved—some of them were Daddy's hired hands.

"What y'all know good?" her father said, rolling down his window and slowing the truck as they neared the men.

"Devil beating his wife today, ain't he?" one of the men said. He grinned. A wide, nearly toothless grin.

Staggerlee smiled, looking out to where the sun had peeked out a bit between two clouds. It was an old expression, one she had heard her father use a couple of times—sun showers meant the devil was beating his wife. It didn't make any sense but it was always funny to hear.

Her father laughed and pulled over.

"We're going to be late," Staggerlee said, getting nervous. "Tyler'll be waiting."

He looked at his watch. "We'll make it, sugar. Let me just say a quick hello."

Another man came up to the truck—a dark, gray-haired man in work pants and a shirt so washed out, Staggerlee couldn't guess what its original color had been.

"Your south field's gonna need plowing before the

41

sun gets too hot, Canan. I got some time next week I could get to it, if you'd like."

"That'd be as good a time as any, Trev. Just come on by and do it and let me know how much you got coming to you."

Trev smiled. "That your baby girl there?"

Daddy nodded.

"How you doing, brown sugar child?"

"Fine, sir."

"She getting big, ain't she?" He turned back to the men. "Y'all see Canan's baby girl—she just about grown, ain't she?"

Staggerlee's face grew hot.

"Look just like he spit her out," another man said.

"Be beating boys off with a stick soon, Canan. My big-headed boy Derrick's in your class, ain't he?" He took a handkerchief from his pocket and dabbed at the rain dripping from his forehead.

"Yes sir." His son was loud and gangly. Once, a few years back, he had put an apple on her desk, with a tiny red heart taped to it. Staggerlee had eaten the apple and returned the red heart. She had no idea what he had intended for her to do with it. After that, he had seemed cold toward her.

"Adeen got another one coming." Her father grinned.

Derrick's father whistled, low and steady, then turned to the group again. "Y'all hear that? Another one coming."

They all hooted.

"Can't keep the rooster in the barn, can you?" Trev grinned.

Daddy smiled, and Trev tapped the truck once and stepped away.

"You give my best to your family," he said as Daddy started the engine. "I'll see y'all sometime next week."

They drove off slowly, Daddy grinning and giving one last wave before he turned at the corner. When he got around his men friends, he seemed to step into a different person—someone relaxed and easygoing and ready to laugh. He had known some of those men all his life. Staggerlee leaned out the window and squinted against the wind. Her mother didn't have this—a group of people to laugh with. She spent most of her time alone or with the family or knitting or reading.

"You think Mama's lonely?" Staggerlee asked, poking her head back in.

Her father glanced at her. "Where'd that come from?"

Staggerlee shrugged. "It's just that you have your menfolk friends in town and Sweet Gum's mostly all black people. Mama doesn't have anyone."

"You think she doesn't have anyone because Sweet Gum is mostly black folk?" Daddy asked, raising an eyebrow.

Staggerlee shrugged again. "I didn't mean that. I mean, she just doesn't have anyone. I don't know if it's about black or white."

Daddy frowned. "Good—'cause it's not. Your mother's always been on solo. And I wouldn't have

43

brought her back to Sweet Gum if she hadn't wanted to come here." He looked over at her.

"She seems so alone, though."

"She is alone. Some people go crazy if they feel like they don't have any type of community or close friends and whatnot. Your mama's not like that. She never did like a big social kind of lifestyle, always preferred to be by herself. Or now, with me and you kids."

"Well, I figure I'd like to have me a good friend in my lifetime."

Daddy patted her leg. "Then you will, Miss Staggerlee. You will."

But she wasn't sure she believed him.

CHAPTER SEVEN

The rain stopped halfway to Tudor. By the time they arrived, the roads were hot and dusty again.

Tudor Station was small—not much more than a storefront with a ticket counter and a dusty red dirt road where Trailways pulled in once a day. Staggerlee climbed down from the truck and looked around at the station. Today it seemed shabby, dusty and bare. She swallowed. What would Tyler think of it?

"I guess she's on her way," she said, brushing off the knees of her overalls and smoothing her ponytail back. Her feet were sweating inside her hiking boots, and she couldn't tell whether it was nervousness or heat.

When the bus pulled in, it took the driver a moment to get the door open. Staggerlee bit her cuticle. She moved a step closer to her father and waited.

Tyler stepped down carrying a duffel bag. The sun was hot and bright now, and she shaded her eyes with her hand and squinted at them—a half smile working one side of her face. Staggerlee felt her mouth go dry.

Tyler was beautiful, like nobody she had ever seen before.

Daddy rushed over, smiling and taking her duffel. "Tyler, I'm your uncle Elijah. Good to see you. Real good!" He gave her a quick hug. "Come meet your cousin, girl."

Staggerlee shoved her hands in her pockets and stared down at her boots. It was the kind of beautiful you couldn't put a finger on. Separately, all the parts of Tyler's face didn't add up to anything. But together they were beautiful. She tried to keep her eyes on her boots, but something kept pulling her gaze back.

"I'm Stag . . . Staggerlee," she said when they walked over.

Tyler gave her a strange look and shifted her knapsack higher onto her shoulder. She was wearing a dungaree jacket with TROUT stitched across one of the pockets. Underneath the jacket, she was all in black.

Staggerlee took a deep breath. "Guess you're Tyler."

Tyler shook her head and raised an eyebrow.

"My name is Trout." Her voice was soft and even. She looked Staggerlee over, and her eyes seemed to click into place as though she had just decided something. She pulled her lips to one side of her face. It made her look older than fourteen. "I thought your name was Evangeline Ian."

Staggerlee hadn't expected her not to have an accent. It sounded strange, how clear her words came out.

"I thought yours was Tyler."

She smiled, and Staggerlee smiled back, kicking one of her hiking boots against a rock.

"Yeah," she said. "Well, Ida and Jonathan tried that name out on me."

They stared at each other, smiling. One of Trout's eyebrows curved into an arch, which made her look skeptical even when she was smiling. Staggerlee remembered all those love-at-first-sight stories she used to read—how she had never believed them. But standing there, in the Tudor bus station, she felt something weird happening inside her stomach and all around her—like something pounding, trying to get out of her. Her mind kept running back to Hazel in those cornflowers.

"Seems neither of you were happy with the names your mamas gave you," Daddy said.

Staggerlee jumped. She had forgotten he was standing there.

He lifted Tyler's duffel into the back of the truck.

"My mother named me Danielle, sir. Ida and Jonathan named me Tyler."

"And you don't consider Ida and Jonathan your people?" Daddy asked. "Because if they're not your people, then what does that make me and this fine daughter of mine, who just drove a good long way to pick up a city-slick niece and cousin we heard was coming in from Baltimore?"

Staggerlee glared at him. He seemed out of place— like a wall between her and Trout.

"Yes, sir," Trout said quietly, glancing away from him. "They're my people. They raised me."

"Well then, Miss Trout Danielle Tyler," Daddy said, "welcome to Calmuth County. My mama, your grandma, named me Elijah and I think I'll hold on to that name awhile."

Trout smiled and followed behind Daddy, taking high steps to keep her shoes from getting covered in red dust.

"It's a losing battle, Trout," Staggerlee said, pointing down at her own hiking boots.

"You always wear those boots?"

"Most of the time."

"They look like it. I brought stuff with me to keep my shoes shined. You can use it if you want. Can we ride in back, Uncle Elijah?" She hoisted her knapsack into the truck.

Staggerlee frowned. Who'd ever heard of shiny hiking boots?

"Probably get a bit windy back there," Daddy said.

"I don't mind." She looked at Staggerlee. "You mind, Staggerlee?"

"No." Maybe Staggerlee would have followed Trout to the end of the world.

"Okay then," Daddy said, climbing into the cab.

Trout climbed into the back easily and scooted to one corner. Staggerlee climbed up after her and settled against a bag of fertilizer her father had picked up in town. Red dust kicked up around the truck as he slowly maneuvered it back onto the main road. Staggerlee tried not to look at Trout, but Trout was looking hard at her, so that every time Staggerlee's eyes slid in Trout's direction, they bumped smack against hers.

Staggerlee started braiding her hair—hoping to keep the wind from whipping it into snarls.

"Don't do that," Trout said. "I like it."

Staggerlee let it drop back into a ponytail.

"Ida said she was sending me here to spend time with some ladies and gentlemen," Trout said above the noise of the truck. "You sure don't look like a lady."

"How's a lady supposed to look?"

Trout shrugged. "How am I supposed to know? I guess liking lipstick and dresses and stuff. Wearing bras. Ida says one day I'm going to be too big for T-shirts. I hope that day isn't planning on coming soon."

"I still wear T-shirts too."

Tyler smiled. "Good. Otherwise, I'd be embarrassed."

"And anyway, Ida never even met us before."

"I know. But we've seen lots of pictures. You know—in newspapers and magazines and stuff."

"Didn't reporters bother you all?" Staggerlee asked.

"Shoot," Trout said. "Once in a blue. They don't care anything about our boring lives. Ida married a college professor. Hallique started a couple of fund-raising organizations for black people—for a while, reporters were into that. But the organizations ran out of money and she went back to her regular life being a secretary. They wanted you guys for the dirt. Look at you—you could pass for white. The press loves that kind of stuff."

Staggerlee looked away. At school she had been called "Light-bright." She hated it, the way the word sounded so much like a swear, how girls' mouths curved so nastily when they screamed it. When she was younger, she hated how light she was, how people stared and called her beautiful or ugly just because of it. Some mornings, she wanted to pull her skin back and walk outside with just her blood and veins and bone showing. What would people say then? What names would they come up with? She looked at Trout. Her skin was dark brown like Daddy's. Staggerlee wanted to touch it, to run her hands along Trout's arm. She wanted to ask her what it was like to walk inside that skin every day.

"Why would I want to pass?" Her voice came out sounding cold. "I know what I am."

Trout narrowed her eyes, smirking. "What are you?"

It was a test, Staggerlee knew. One she had had to take a thousand times. Choose a side, Trout was saying. Black or white.

"I'm me. That's all."

Trout's eyes softened. Staggerlee stared into them. They were brown and clear as water.

"Yeah," Trout said. "I hear that." She turned away from Staggerlee and watched the passing land for a while, squinting against the dust. "That's all anybody is—themselves. People all the time wanting to change that."

She looked old sitting there, all huddled into her jacket.

"Are you glad you came here?"

Trout looked thoughtful a moment. "I don't know yet." She sighed. "I miss Hallique." For a minute she looked like she'd start crying. But then she blinked and her eyes were distant again.

Staggerlee leaned back and stared out over the land. The pictures they had of her father's people had been taken a long time ago. In most of them, Hallique and Ida were little girls, and there were a few of them as teenagers. Hallique never smiled in any of the pictures. When Staggerlee had asked her father why, he'd said, "That's how she was—straight-faced."

"What do you miss about her?" Staggerlee asked Trout now.

Trout shrugged. "I look over at her chair at the table and it's empty and I know it'll always be empty now. And her pictures. I look at them and . . . I don't know. She's there in them but she's not, too." She reached into her knapsack and pulled out a small stack of pictures with a rubber band around it.

"We went to the shore last year." She handed the picture to Staggerlee. "This is me and Hallique."

Staggerlee stared at the picture a long time. The woman in it was tall and dark like Daddy. Her hair was braided and pinned to the top of her head. She wore tiny wire-frame glasses and had an arm across Trout's shoulder. They were both laughing into the camera.

"That's Hallique?" Staggerlee asked softly.

"Yeah."

"I never saw a picture with her smiling." She stared at the picture again. They were both wearing shorts. Trout was wearing an orange bathing suit beneath hers. Hallique wore a T-shirt with something written across it Staggerlee couldn't read.

"She said when she was young, she was too busy worrying about what her life was gonna be like when

51

she grew up. But after the bombing, she said she was going to live—that tomorrow wasn't guaranteed." Tyler frowned. "Or something like that."

"Then why'd she stop talking to Daddy, if she was going to *live*?"

Trout shrugged. "She never talked about that. Neither one of them did. It was like your daddy was dead and buried. Hardly any pictures either—except what they clipped from the newspaper."

"They hated us."

"They didn't hate you. They just didn't think about you all. I guess that's just as bad, huh?"

Staggerlee nodded. "Somebody dies and then everyone scrambles to make things right."

Trout raised her eyebrow. "What're you talking about?"

"Like Ida Mae letting us finally meet you. Finally writing to us. It took somebody dying."

"Yeah," Trout said, looking away from her. "Somebody dying." She got quiet, and Staggerlee wondered what she had said wrong.

"Anyway, Hallique smiled all the time," Trout said. "I think that's what I'll miss the most. The way she laughed at Jonathan's silly jokes. I think I was closest to Hallique. I could tell her anything." Trout looked down at the stack. "Ida Mae's not like that. Ida Mae's got big plans for me."

She held out another picture. "That's them. Ida and Jonathan."

Staggerlee stared at the picture a moment. Ida Mae was short and round. She was waving the camera away the way Mama did sometimes when she had had enough picture taking. But Jonathan was holding her by the shoulders, playfully, as though he was making her stand still for one more. He was handsome, younger than Staggerlee had expected him to be.

"They're good-looking," Staggerlee said finally, handing the picture back.

Trout nodded. "I know, and I know I don't look like them either."

"You're good-looking," Staggerlee said quickly.

Trout smiled and winked at her. Something about the wink made Staggerlee's stomach flutter.

They were driving through Calmuth. The land stretched out green and gold in the sun. Trout leaned back against the cab. "It's pretty here."

"Baltimore pretty?"

Trout sat up. "You know why Ida is sending me here?"

Staggerlee frowned. "You wanted to come!"

"Is that what she said in her letters?"

"Yeah. Didn't you want to come? To meet us?"

Trout leaned back again, looking relieved and pent up at the same time. "It's bigger than that," she sighed.

Trout looked at her a moment, as though she was trying to figure out if Staggerlee would understand something. Then she shook her head.

"Bigger than what?" Staggerlee asked.

"Nothing," Trout said.

Staggerlee took her harmonica out of her back pocket and started blowing into it. The music surrounded them. She felt scared suddenly that Trout had brought something deep with her, something that concerned both of them. Trout made her feel small and shaky. And her lips were scary, the way they curved into a smile.

Staggerlee started playing "Moonlight in Vermont." Over and over she had watched the film clip of her grandmother singing it with Ella Fitzgerald. Their voices together were beautiful. Later in the song, a man came out and started playing the trumpet. Staggerlee played that part now. She felt herself disappearing inside the music.

" 'Moonlight in Vermont . . . ,' " Trout began to sing.

Staggerlee frowned, unsure whether or not she had heard right. She had never heard anyone but her grandmother and Ella sing the song, and now here was Trout. She began to play more softly. Trout smiled and continued singing, her voice sweet and low. She sang with her eyes closed, her head thrown back. Staggerlee stared at her mouth, the way it moved to form the words. She felt her throat closing up, felt tears beginning to form behind her eyes. She stopped playing suddenly and stared down at her harmonica.

"Why'd you stop?"

"How do you know that song?"

Trout frowned. "The same way you do, silly. Grandma sang it. We have it on video."

They had the same grandmother. Georgia Canan. Somehow that seemed strange to Staggerlee, that this Trout shared her grandmother.

"We have it on video too," Staggerlee said.

Trout stared out at the passing road, smiling. "I like

when she and Ella do that little step," she said, moving her shoulders. "And then they go 'Oooh oooh oooh. Ooooh.' I love that."

Staggerlee smiled. She loved that part too.

"You ever been there—to Vermont?"

Trout shook her head. "I dreamed it, though—when I was real little, I used to have all these ideas about—about what it was like. The way Grandma sings it—that part about the falling leaves and the sycamores."

"And the snowlight," Staggerlee said softly. "Sometimes I sit in my window and imagine what that's like—snowlight and ski trails." All her life, she had felt like she was the only one who dreamed about places. The only one who watched those film clips and imagined herself in the places they sang about. And now, here was the girl—sitting close enough to touch, talking about the same things.

"And I know why you call yourself Staggerlee too."

Staggerlee started picking at a cuticle. It was almost too much—like Trout could look right through her and see everything. "Why do you think?"

" 'Cause of Grandpa's song," she said, matter-of-fact.

"Yeah," she said. But it was more than that. Nothing she could explain to a near stranger. "How come you call yourself Trout?"

They passed a farm where about a dozen cows were out grazing. Trout watched them, her eyes on the farm until it was long out of sight. "You ever been fishing?" she said, finally.

"No. I watch people do it. We have a river near us."

"When I was little, Jonathan used to take me fishing all the time. We don't do it much anymore, though. Ida says he should take my boy cousins fishing and leave me to do girl stuff. Thing is—we used to fish for trout. You ever see a trout getting pulled out of water?"

Staggerlee shook her head. Once she had seen a man hit a fish against the ground so hard it brought tears to her eyes. It was a bluefish about as long as her arm. Since then, she always looked away when a person had a fish on their line.

"A trout will fight you real hard," Trout said. "Trying to get itself free. I'd get one on the line and it'd be leaping all high out of the water." She sighed. "Sometimes I'd keep it. Sometimes I'd let it go. But even when I let it go, I'd think about its mouth, the way it had this big cut in there—the way I'd hurt it even if I did throw it back."

"How come you liked fishing if you didn't like hurting them?"

Trout looked at her, her eyes dark and intense. "Something about the way they fought. I guess, without even knowing it, I wanted to learn how to fight like that. I wanted to see this little fish that thought he had so much to live for. That's why I changed my name. Be a fighter like a trout. You give yourself a name, you have to live up to it, though."

"You feel like you have to fight all the time?"

Trout looked away. "Yeah," she said. "All the time."

She was quiet, her eyes steady on the land they passed. Staggerlee sat holding her ponytail, trying to keep the wind from whipping it into her face. She watched Trout. Her jaw was narrow and strong. It looked like someone had chiseled it out of a piece of dark brown stone. But her chin kept quivering as though she was trying hard not to cry. They drove for a long time before the first tear fell. Trout wiped it away quickly.

"Don't stare at me, please," she said hoarsely.

They rode the rest of the way in silence.

CHAPTER EIGHT

At the house Trout slowly climbed down from the truck and moved toward the porch where Mama was standing with Battle. She walked like someone older, someone sure of herself. Staggerlee watched them embrace awkwardly, then pull away from each other and smile. Her mother's smile was small and uncertain.

"I hope you have a good time here," Mama said. But her words sounded as though she had practiced saying them.

"I'll show her a good time," Staggerlee said quickly.

Trout turned and looked at her, a half smile beginning. Staggerlee frowned. She didn't have words for this—the way Trout . . . the way Trout . . . unsteadied her.

She took Trout's duffel from her father. "I—I'll show you where you're sleeping," she stammered.

TROUT'S ROOM WAS next to Staggerlee's, and even though it was called a guest room, there had

58

never been a guest in it. Staggerlee looked around. Her mother had slept here. When she had returned from the hospital after having Battle, she had moved into this room and closed the door. And for the next few weeks, they tiptoed around the house, only disturbing her when it was time for Battle to nurse or on the few occasions when she herself was hungry. The room was painted blue, with a high ceiling and windows facing the river. There was a queen-sized iron bed in one corner, a desk with a lamp on it in the other, and a small blue-and-yellow rug on the floor.

"This is it," Staggerlee said, setting Trout's duffel on the bed.

Trout whistled under her breath and walked over to the window. She stood there, staring out, her hands in the back pockets of her shorts.

"Something sad about this room."

"Sad," Staggerlee repeated softly. She remembered how she would tiptoe down the hall and peek in on her mother, who lay sleeping. How bright the room was in the mornings, the yellow-gold light making her mother seem almost holy.

"I don't think it's sad." She sat down on the edge of the bed and fingered the patchwork quilt. "Our grandmother made this."

Trout turned away from the window. She looked at the quilt a moment and nodded. "I know how to do that kind of piecework. Ida Mae taught me."

"I'd like to learn one day," Staggerlee said. "Mama knits but she doesn't know anything about quilting."

Trout smiled. She had the prettiest smile. *Laugh for me,* Staggerlee wanted to say.

"I thought I was going to hate quilting at first, but it's like . . . it's like you take all these pieces from all these parts of your life and you sew them together and then you have your life all over again, only it's . . . in a different form." Trout turned back to the window. "I don't know if that makes any sense."

"Yeah. It does."

"What's that water?" Trout asked.

"Breakabone River. Daddy says it got its name because so many slaves broke their bones trying to swim it to freedom."

Staggerlee started chewing on a cuticle. Mama hated when she did this. She stopped as though Mama had just fussed at her for it. She wanted words—the way Trout had them—for every feeling, it seemed, every thought.

"Ida Mae didn't send me here because I wanted to come," Trout said softly. "She sent me here because she doesn't like the person I'm growing up to be."

Staggerlee stared out the window past Trout. The sun was setting now, beautiful and clear across the water.

"Who?" She felt her knees trembling and put her hands on them to steady them. "Who are you growing up to be?"

Trout looked at her a long time. She came over to the bed and sat down beside Staggerlee. It felt strange having her so close. She smelled of lotion. Staggerlee wanted to put her nose in Trout's hair and sniff hard.

"Look at this," Trout said. She spread her hand out next to Staggerlee's and stared at them. Trout's skin was dark reddish brown. Staggerlee's hand looked pale beside it. "Look at how different we are."

"It's just skin," Staggerlee said. They were sitting shoulder to shoulder. They were whispering now.

Trout looked at her and smiled. "Can we walk down to the river later?"

Staggerlee nodded and stood up quickly before Trout could tell her what terrible thing she'd done to get sent here by Ida Mae.

"I should let you . . . get settled," she said, moving toward the door. Her legs seemed to be disconnected from the rest of her.

"Will you come get me later?" Trout asked.

Staggerlee nodded and pulled Trout's door closed behind her.

CHAPTER NINE

She had always come to the barn. When she was little, her parents would find her here, curled up on a bale of hay, her harmonica lying at her side. A long time ago, when Dotti still came here to groom her horse, Buck, Staggerlee would tag along behind her and beg until Dotti lifted her up onto Buck's back and taught her to ride. But Dotti outgrew Buck, and Staggerlee didn't care enough about riding to take him over. The morning her father sold him, Staggerlee had come to the barn to pack up his brushes and saddle and say goodbye. And Buck had looked at her with milky eyes. Each time Staggerlee slid the heavy door open and stepped into the empty barn, she remembered him.

When she was ten she found a litter of motherless kittens in the barn. For weeks the family nursed them, with tiny bottles and kitten formula her father had gotten in town. Staggerlee sat in the dim barn remembering them all sitting in a semicircle, each with a kitten in their lap. They had kept one—Mamie, a calico. Staggerlee pressed her harmonica to her lips and remembered people calling to adopt the others, until one by one, they were gone.

She sat cross-legged in the center of the barn now, Buck's scratchy blue blanket pulled across her shoulders, and played softly. When she was eleven, she would come here late at night and stare through the barn's cutout window up at the moon. She dreamed of flying Daddy's planes and making enough money to buy more harmonicas. Enough to last her forever. Staggerlee smiled, remembering. She used to imagine traveling around the world and finding all the people in it who loved to be alone, who loved the sound of music. And she would start a small band and build lots of barns far apart from each other. And she and the other musicians would sit in the darkness of their individual barns and play, listening to each other, and the music would travel up through the windows and meet the moon.

Staggerlee blew softly into the harmonica. She licked her lips and started playing, her eyes half closed, her head moving slowly from side to side. She remembered the feel of Trout's shoulder pressed against hers and the way Trout's lips moved when she spoke. But out here playing, Staggerlee wasn't afraid of Trout. She felt far away and safe. She felt free.

CHAPTER TEN

Over the next few days, Mama and Trout moved carefully around each other. Sometimes, sitting at dinner, Trout would say something that made Mama smile. In those moments, Staggerlee felt like her heart would break open. Her mother didn't smile much, and the scarce times when her face lit up were amazing. Maybe Trout felt it too. She started talking more and more after a while, telling funny stories about Baltimore and her family. One night, Staggerlee caught Trout staring at Mama, watching the way she lifted a slice of corn bread to her mouth, and she knew in that moment that Trout had begun to look past all the mean things Ida Mae must have said about them.

"Did our grandparents love you?" Trout asked one evening at dinner.

"What kind of question is that?" Dotti asked, nearly choking on her rice.

Trout glared at her, then turned back to Mama. Staggerlee smiled.

"We never met," Mama said. "Ida Mae never told you?"

Trout shook her head, not taking her eyes off Mama.

"Elijah and I had planned to come at the end of the summer of sixty-nine. He had written them about us and they had written back saying they were looking forward to meeting me."

"They died that summer," Trout said.

Mama nodded and pushed some peas around on her plate.

"They would have loved you," Staggerlee said.

Mama smiled. "I like to *think* so."

Her father had been sitting quietly, his hand pressed against his mouth, his thick brows furrowed.

"That's what they lived for," he said. "They would've gotten to know you." He smiled. "I'm sure my mother wouldn't have thought anyone was good enough for her baby boy, but she would've given anyone who tried to be a chance—black or white."

Trout was staring down at her plate. "I try to think about how they were regular people," she said. "That's what everybody seems to want to forget."

Staggerlee swallowed, wanting to reach under the table, take her hand, and squeeze it hard. She knew what Trout was talking about. Everyone had gone and made their grandparents heroes. There was a statue of them up in town. Her grandfather held a Bible in his hand and her grandmother held a poster that said WE WHO BELIEVE IN FREEDOM SHALL NOT REST. They were heroes. But they were also human. And because nobody wanted to believe that, it was hard for people to see any of the Canans as human. Including her and Trout.

"I mean—what if they wouldn't have liked you?" Trout said.

"That's just dumb." Dotti glared at Trout. "You don't know anything about them."

Trout's eyes didn't flicker from Mama.

Staggerlee watched Dotti, who was looking at Trout out of the corner of her eye, as though she was waiting for Trout to pull something. Trout ignored her, and this burned Dotti up more than anything.

Mama nodded. "You're right," she said. "It's easy to imagine them only as heroes. Sometimes people need the easy way."

Daddy pushed his plate away and leaned back. "I don't think my parents had that kind of hate in them," he said. "I think I would have inherited at least some of it."

"But look at Ida Mae," Trout said. "She's—"

"Can I be excused?" Dotti interrupted.

"Whose night for dishes?" Daddy asked.

"Go," Staggerlee said. "It's my night. Goodbye."

"I'll help you," Trout offered.

"Dotti, help Battle to bed," Mama said. "Make sure he brushes his teeth." Dotti scowled, mumbling as she lifted Battle from his high chair. The dining room seemed to get lighter after she left.

"Ida Mae's from the same people," Trout continued as though she hadn't been interrupted. "And she'd never go out and marry a white guy."

66

"Why does it matter?" Mama said, annoyed.

Trout slunk down a bit in her chair. "I was just wondering," she said. "Just trying to figure it all out."

Mama reached across the table and put her hand on Trout's shoulder. "No one person ever figures it all out, honey."

Trout shrugged. "Maybe I'll be the first."

CHAPTER ELEVEN

"You ready for our walk by the river?" Staggerlee asked the next morning. Downstairs, she could hear Dotti clearing away the breakfast dishes.

Trout was sitting on her bed lacing her sneaker. She was dressed in black again, and Staggerlee wondered if everything she owned was black.

"I dreamed about the river last night." Trout smiled. She had combed her hair back from her face and tied it with a ribbon. "I dreamed about bones floating in it. People's bones."

"The slaves probably," Staggerlee said. She leaned against the doorway and watched Trout. "Sorry Dotti's kind of rude."

Trout rolled her eyes. "She's got her own thing going on. That's fine with me." She started making her bed.

"You don't have to do that now," Staggerlee said.

"Yes I do. Ida Mae said it's good home training—to make your bed before you go off on your day. I'm not going to leave it unmade so you all can talk about me when I'm gone."

She looked over her shoulder at Staggerlee and smiled.

"We wouldn't talk about you."

"You won't have anything to talk about." When she finished, she turned. She was serious again, and Staggerlee felt her stomach flutter. "In that dream, those bones seemed to be calling my name."

"Your name?"

"Yeah." Trout paused. "I need to tell you something, Stag. I need to tell you why Ida Mae sent me here. If we're going to be friends, I don't want it starting out on a lie."

"I don't know if it's something I want to hear."

Trout stared at her a long time. "If you don't want me to tell you . . . I won't."

But Staggerlee knew why Ida Mae had sent Trout here; she could see it in Trout's eyes and she could feel it when Trout sat down next to her. There was a feeling growing inside Trout, and Staggerlee knew it because it was growing inside her too. Maybe it had always been there. Maybe it had started before she was born and would keep growing—into the earth—long after she had died. She knew it was secret and shameful. When Mama had given her a taste of wine for becoming a woman, she knew that was different somehow—that the woman thing happened to every girl and because of this, they could celebrate it. But what was happening to her and Trout—that was different. They were alone together. There was no one standing behind a closed door smiling and holding out a glass of wine.

"I know why, Trout," Staggerlee whispered.

Trout ran her hand slowly back and forth over the quilt. "How come you know?"

Staggerlee shrugged. She had never spoken about it and couldn't now. She didn't have the words for any of it, but her feelings were like words inside her—painful and sharp.

"I just do," she said finally.

She could see Trout swallow. "Ida Mae thinks I could learn to be a lady here."

Staggerlee smiled, and the air grew lighter. "Lady. Sounds like something out of the eighteen-hundreds."

"I think that's when Ida Mae should have been born." Trout looked down at her hands. "Hallique understood me. I could tell her anything and she didn't judge it. When she was dying, she called Ida Mae into the room and told her to be patient with me, to give me some growing room. I was standing outside the bedroom door listening." She blinked and wiped her eyes with the back of her hand. "Then she told Ida Mae why she needed to be patient with me and Ida Mae lost it. She just lost it."

Staggerlee had run home from that afternoon in the cornflowers with Hazel bursting to tell someone. But as she got closer to the house, she slowed down. Somehow she knew there was no one—no one who would say "That's wonderful that someone made you so happy."

"She said when I come home from here," Trout was saying, "all these feelings I have better be gone. Feels like everyone in my life has betrayed me." She looked over at Staggerlee. "I guess I'm kind of scared you will too."

CHAPTER TWELVE

They spent their first few weeks together walking along the Breakabone River, Creek barking and dancing around them. And in the blue heat of summer, Staggerlee fell in love with Trout's voice, soft against the rush of the river. Around them, pecan and sweet gum trees blossomed and swayed. In the late afternoon, they picked azaleas and Indian paintbrush and mountain laurel for the dinner table.

Some evenings, Trout asked to be alone and went out walking. Those times, Staggerlee watched from her window until Trout became tiny in the distance and faded into the line of evergreens. Those times, Staggerlee felt her heart caving in around itself.

She had dreamed Trout before she came. Dreamed a girl who would be like her—liking the same things, knowing the same history. Someone her age who she'd walk along the Breakabone River with. She had dreamed them sitting on the porch laughing together. Dreamed the red dust rising up around them as they walked. Each time Trout left to go off on her own,

Staggerlee thought about the day Trout would go off for good.

Some evenings, the phone would ring. And when the answering machine clicked on, there was a girl's voice on the other end, asking for Trout. When Trout ran for the phone, Staggerlee longed to run after her, to sit beside her and listen. But she didn't. Instead, she sat on her hands and waited. When Trout hung up, she was often quiet. She seemed younger after those phone calls—less sure of herself. Staggerlee watched her, wondering what the girl had said to make her feel this way.

ONE MORNING ABOUT a month after Trout arrived, Staggerlee woke up to find her standing in the doorway. It was dawn, and gray light trickled in from the shutters Staggerlee had pulled closed the night before.

"Your dog always sleep right next to your bed like that?" Trout whispered, sitting down at the foot of the bed. Creek lifted his head and yawned. He was curled up on his dog bed, a round dark blue mat Daddy had made.

Staggerlee squinted up at her. It felt strange to wake to Trout in the room sitting cross-legged at the foot of her bed.

"The floors are cold here," Trout said. She was barefoot, dressed in dark pajamas. She had braided her hair, and the braids hung down beside her ears.

Staggerlee sat up, pulling the covers with her. Creek

sat up too, went over to Trout, and rested his head on her lap. She stroked it slowly.

"How long were you standing there—in the doorway like that?"

Trout shrugged. "A little while—maybe twenty minutes. I was watching you sleep. You're pretty when you're sleeping. So peaceful."

"That's weird to me." Staggerlee frowned. "You standing there." It gave her the creeps to think of someone watching her when she didn't know they were there. "Do you always watch people like that?"

"I had a bad dream. I dreamed I didn't have a family. I was standing out in this field and there was all this snow around and I just kept calling everybody's name. People I knew kept turning and looking at me like I was some kind of crazy stranger."

"They probably just thought you were some kind of crazy," Staggerlee said, wiping sleep out of her eyes. "They probably knew you were going to be standing in my door in the next minute staring at me."

"You were there," Trout said. "You walked right by me."

Staggerlee looked at her. "It was a dream, Trout."

"When I'm walking in the woods sometimes, my mind is all filled up thinking about you, Staggerlee."

Staggerlee shivered and pulled the covers tighter around her.

"Have you ever kissed anyone?"

"Once," Staggerlee said softly, looking away from Trout. "I kissed a girl once."

She had never even said this out loud.

74

"What happened?"

"She found a way to never speak to me again."

"I used to tell Hallique everything," Trout said softly. "The first time I kissed a girl, I told her." She crawled up beside Staggerlee and climbed under the covers. Staggerlee moved over to make space for her. "She said that I'd get crushes on lots of people, boys and girls." Trout frowned. "I asked her . . . I said . . . , 'But what if I always want this?' "

"Did she say it was bad?" Staggerlee asked. She could feel Trout's leg pressed against hers. She wanted to push it away. She wanted to pull it closer.

Trout shook her head. "She just said it was something I should keep to myself."

"But she told Ida Mae."

Trout turned toward the window. Staggerlee could see the outline of her throat moving up and down. "I know," she said softly. "And then she died before I could get mad at her."

"Nobody ever told me I had to hide it," Staggerlee said. "I think I just told myself. I read this book once where this woman fell in love with another woman and she couldn't deal with it so she jumped off this cliff. It scared me. I hadn't thought about it again until I kissed—I kissed Hazel."

"Where'd you find a book like that?"

"It was this old book. I was into reading stuff written a long time ago. I didn't even know what it was about until I got halfway through it."

"You think your parents would still love you?" Trout asked.

"I don't know. I really don't."

Trout rested her head on Staggerlee's shoulder. "But one day you're going to find out."

They didn't say anything for a long time. The sun was almost up now. Staggerlee watched the dust-filled rays seep through the shutters. She could not believe she had told someone about Hazel. She could not believe how easy it had been, how safe it felt.

"Who's that girl who calls you, Trout?"

Trout sighed. "That's my friend Rachel. She's on a mission to find me a boyfriend."

"I thought it was your girlfriend."

Trout laughed. "Oh God—Rachel would drop dead standing if she heard that. Every time she calls, it's to tell me about some guy or some party she went to and all the guys that were into her there." She turned to Staggerlee. "Sometimes I want that, though—to just be able to walk out into the world and *be*. I couldn't imagine going to some party with a girl as my date."

"Why not?"

Trout shrugged. "I guess I'm just . . . I don't know— I don't have what it would take. To have people pointing and laughing, that would kill me. Would you do it?"

Staggerlee nodded. "If I loved someone enough, I would go anywhere in the world with them." She thought about Hazel. She would've walked off the end of the world with her and not cared about anyone saying anything. Maybe that's what she should have told Hazel that morning in the schoolyard.

"That's good that you have that in you. I think some

people can do it and some people can't. I wish I was one of the ones who had that kind of . . . of whatever it is, in me."

"Maybe you'll have it one day. Maybe it comes later on for some people."

Trout shook her head and smiled.

"I'd never leave you standing in a field, Trout. If you called my name, I'd answer."

"I know."

"I'd say 'Hey, Trout. What you know good? Where you been, girl?' "

"And I'd say 'Hey, Staggerlee, It's been a long time.' " Trout sounded groggy.

"I'd like that," Staggerlee said softly. "I'd like to have someone else like me somewhere in the world."

But Trout's breath was coming soft and even, and Staggerlee knew she had fallen asleep.

CHAPTER THIRTEEN

When Trout came downstairs the next morning, Staggerlee was dressing Battle. He smiled when he saw her.

"Hey, Battle," Trout said, bending down to kiss him.

"Dotti's taking him out with her today—visiting," Staggerlee said, lacing his shoe. She felt nervous suddenly. Last night had almost seemed like a dream, and she wondered how much Trout remembered. "I have to clean the kitchen. Mama's not feeling so well. We left some breakfast out for you."

Trout looked at her without smiling.

"What?" Staggerlee said.

"Nothing."

Dotti came down the stairs and lifted Battle into her arms. She and Trout exchanged looks.

"Hey, Trout. How's it going?"

"Fine, thanks."

Trout looked down at her hands and continued staring at them until Dotti and Battle were gone.

"She makes me feel weird," Trout said in the kitchen. Staggerlee set a plate of toast and eggs in front of her.

"That's just Dotti. I think she practices that in the mirror—seeing how weird she can make people feel."

Trout ate slowly. "Sorry I woke you up last night like that."

"That's okay."

Trout chewed a piece of toast. She ate delicately, carefully. "Hallique was the only one I've ever told anything to. It feels weird this morning now."

"I never told anybody," Staggerlee said softly.

"Nobody?"

Staggerlee shook her head and smiled.

"Geez."

"It feels good, though." Staggerlee looked at her. "I mean, I feel—relieved, I guess. Like I'm not walking around anymore with this thing I can't tell anyone."

"You never told *anyone*?"

Staggerlee shook her head, then got up and started clearing the table. Trout took a last bite of egg and rose to help her. Staggerlee felt lighter this morning, happier than she'd felt in a long time.

"Not even your best friend?"

"I don't have a best friend," Staggerlee said quietly. The words embarrassed her suddenly. "I don't really—" She turned to Trout, and the look in Trout's eyes made her stop midsentence. Trout's look said she was coming to some deep conclusion about Staggerlee. "Nothing."

"Why not?"

Staggerlee turned back to the sink. The light feeling she'd had a moment before was gone. She felt like a freak now.

"I just never did."

"Is it because of them?" Trout pointed to a picture of their grandparents. Staggerlee stared at it a long time, then shook her head. "I don't think so. People act weird about them. But I don't know if that's it. At school they say I'm stuck-up. You think I'm stuck-up?"

Trout shrugged. "I don't know you at school. You don't seem stuck-up to me here."

"I just never had a close friend."

Trout hip-checked her and smiled. "Before me."

Staggerlee laughed then and started running water into the sink. "Yeah," she said.

THEY WERE QUIET walking out to the river. Trout had her hands in her pockets. She was wearing her loafers again and taking high steps to keep the dirt off them. Staggerlee smiled.

"I told you it was a losing battle."

Finally Trout took the shoes off and tucked them under her arm.

She looked out over the water. The sun was pretty today, faint and orange in the sky. "Last night when Rachel called—it was to tell me about this guy Matthew who keeps asking her all these questions about me. She set up a date for when I get home."

"Are you going?"

Trout nodded. "I don't really know why I even said I would, but I did. She makes it sound so great—like everything's so much fun." She frowned. "I tell Rachel all this stuff but—like we'll be sitting in my room and she'll be telling me everything about some boy who she thinks she's in love with. It makes me feel awful. Sometimes I even make up some stupid boy. And later, I'll lie in bed thinking how bad it feels—to have to lie to someone like that."

Staggerlee squinted, thinking. "I don't understand it," she said. "No one ever told me I had to lie about it or had to keep it quiet, but somehow I just knew." She brushed her hair back from her face with her hand. "I have all this stuff—all these thoughts going on inside me and they all seem so—so dangerous."

"I see guys in Baltimore wearing these pink triangle pins and I know it's about . . . about being gay," Trout said. They stopped walking and sat down beneath the shade of a sycamore tree.

"Gay," Staggerlee said softly.

They stared out at the water. Staggerlee felt the word settling inside her. It felt too big, somehow.

"I don't know that's what I am, Trout."

Trout frowned. "If you like kissing girls that's what you are."

Staggerlee shivered and wrapped her arms around herself. "It sounds so final. I mean—we're only fourteen."

Trout nodded. She picked up a stick and started scratching their names in the dirt. *Staggerlee and Trout were here today. Maybe they will and maybe they won't be gay.*

Staggerlee read it over her shoulder and smiled.

Trout picked up one of her loafers and started rubbing it out.

"Why are you doing that?"

"I don't want anyone to find it and get stupid."

Staggerlee watched her a moment. "You think the day'll come when you can write something like that in the dirt and it won't faze anybody?"

Trout smiled and started writing their names again. "Guess it won't ever come if it doesn't start someplace, right?"

CHAPTER FOURTEEN

The summer moved past them slowly. Each morning, after cooking and cleaning, they walked down to the river, their fingers laced, Creek dancing around them. On hot afternoons, they pulled their shirts up and pressed their bare stomachs into the cool earth.

They were left alone. Each morning, Staggerlee's father went to the airport. His hired hands moved slowly through the fields, watering and feeding the crops there. Some afternoons, Staggerlee and Trout joined them in the fields and sat listening to the men's tall tales of fifty-pound fish they had almost caught in the Breakabone River and money they would one day make. And once, when they had fallen asleep among the tall stalks of corn, Staggerlee and Trout woke to hear the men laughing and telling stories about different women they had loved.

And in the late afternoon, they would sit on

the porch, drinking lemonade from tall sweating glasses while, upstairs, Staggerlee's mother rested, a book propped against her growing stomach.

"I miss Charlie Horse," Staggerlee said one afternoon as she and Trout sat going through old photo albums. "I think he's the one I'm closest to."

"You don't really like Dotti," Trout said. "I can tell."

Staggerlee looked out over the field. Early each morning, Dotti left on her bike. Some mornings she took Battle with her. Staggerlee knew where she went—into town to sit at the drugstore drinking milk shakes and giggling over boys with her friends.

"Dotti and me—we're real different, I guess."

She pressed her nose into Trout's hair. It smelled of coconut oil.

Trout lifted her head and looked at her.

"I like the way it smells," Staggerlee said, smiling.

Trout ran her hand across Staggerlee's cheek. "Are we gonna stay close? You think we'll always be friends?"

In a week Trout would be leaving. Way too soon.

"Of course." Staggerlee moved closer to her.

"I don't want you to come to the bus station with me. I think it'd be too hard."

Staggerlee nodded.

"I want to remember you like this, sitting on this porch waving goodbye to me." Trout smiled. There were tears standing in her eyes. "I want to remember us together—always."

"You promised to come back here next summer."

"And you promised to write and call."

Staggerlee nodded and put her head on Trout's shoulder. "We still have a week, Trout. Let's not talk about leaving anymore."

CHAPTER FIFTEEN

It rained the morning Staggerlee showed Trout the barn—a cold late-summer rain that seemed to turn the whole world gray. Staggerlee opened the door slowly, soaking and out of breath. They had run barefoot from the house, and Trout pushed past her out of the rain.

"You're shivering," Staggerlee said. The barn was cold and damp. She found the blue blanket and draped it around Trout's shoulders. Trout's teeth chattered, but she was smiling.

"All summer long you never brought me here. I always wondered what this place was."

"My place," Staggerlee said, climbing underneath the blanket with Trout. They sat huddled into each other watching the rain crash down through the barn's high window.

"I come here when I want to be alone. I wanted you to see it, though—so when you go back to Baltimore, you can remember me here, playing music." Staggerlee took out her harmonica and started playing "Moonlight in Vermont."

Trout listened awhile. Then she started singing. And Staggerlee's mind raced back to that first day, in the back of Daddy's truck, the first time she'd heard Trout's voice coming clear and beautiful over her music. They would say goodbye here, Staggerlee knew. In two days, Trout would be gone. In another week, school would start. She pressed closer into Trout. She wanted to remember this moment, remember this feeling, remember Trout.

CHAPTER SIXTEEN

School started on a clear day at the end of August, and Staggerlee took to walking the six miles rather than riding the bus on pretty days. She realized, when she saw students from the year before, that she had grown taller over the summer. Some people waved and smiled, and Staggerlee waved back. Something was different at Sweet Gum High. Or maybe she was different. People spoke to her—said, "Hey, Staggerlee, what you know good?" as though they didn't remember the year before, in middle school, when they had been silent around her. Or maybe it was she who had been silent around them. When Staggerlee found herself smiling at people in the hall, the action felt unfamiliar, and she wondered what her face had been like last year—had she never smiled or said hello? She remembered walking with her head down, watching her feet move one in front of the other, her books clutched to her chest. But she didn't walk that way anymore—she looked ahead of her now, the way Trout had said she should. *Look forward,* Trout had said one afternoon. *Don't you want to see what you're headed for?* Staggerlee smiled. Around her, students were making their way into the building. She could see Dotti at the other end of the stairs, laughing with a group of girls. When Dotti saw her she waved, and Staggerlee waved back. Someone held the door open for her. She thanked him and stepped inside the building.

Hope was born in September. It was warm and clear the day Mama and Daddy returned from the hospital with her. She had been an easy birth, coming quickly in the middle of the day, and Mama seemed rested and happier than she'd been in a long time.

"This is it," Mama said, sitting down heavily. "She's beautiful and sweet and the last Canan baby *I'm* giving birth to."

Daddy smiled and hugged her, then looked over his shoulder to wink at Staggerlee.

They were sitting in the living room, Battle jumping up and down at Staggerlee's side to get a better look at the baby. Late-afternoon sun poured in from the windows, and Mama looked beautiful in it—flushed and golden.

"You make beautiful babies, Mama," Dotti said. "Might as well fill the world with them."

Mama laughed and shook her head.

Hope stared up at Staggerlee, her eyes barely opened. She was pale and bald the way Battle had been. She would darken the way the rest of them had. Maybe her nose would grow straight like Mama's. And her lips fill out like Daddy's.

"Hey, little sister," Staggerlee whispered. "Welcome to Sweet Gum."

That evening, while Mama and Hope slept and Daddy sat in his study reading, Staggerlee called Trout. She had not spoken to her in a week, and her fingers trembled with the excitement of telling her about Hope.

The phone rang twice before Trout picked it up.

"Hey, girl," she said softly. "Goodness, I was just thinking about you."

Staggerlee smiled. They had spoken often since Trout had left, and each time she called, Trout always swore she had just been thinking about her.

"The baby came," Staggerlee said. "We're calling her Hope."

"Hope," Trout said across the distance. "That's pretty. Hope Canan. Cousin Hope Canan."

And they talked long into the night.

CHAPTER SEVENTEEN

Winter came early. By the end of October there was a sprinkling of snow on the ground. Staggerlee walked through it slowly, heading home. In music class, she had sung "I Wonder as I Wander," and her music teacher, Ms. Gibson, had asked if she would join the choir. Staggerlee smiled, remembering the teacher's breathless excitement. "I remember your grandmother," Ms. Gibson had said. "You have her gift of song." Staggerlee had never thought she had anybody's gift of anything. *They're all inside of us,* Staggerlee thought as she climbed the porch stairs, *past people and present people. And probably even the people we'll become.*

She had not heard from Trout in a while. Each time she called, the answering machine picked up. Trout hadn't returned any of her calls. Staggerlee climbed the porch stairs slowly, wondering if she'd done something wrong, and tried to think back to their last conversation. Trout had seemed distant but still Trout, and they had talked about school mostly and a little bit about last summer.

Mama was sitting in the living room nursing Hope. She smiled when Staggerlee came in and blew her a kiss.

"Any calls or letters, Mama?"

"Your friend Lilly called—said meet her downtown by the movie theater if you still want to go see the film."

"Thanks—I'll probably pass."

"Between you and Dotti, it'll soon be time to get another phone line."

"I doubt it," Staggerlee said. But maybe it was true. She had made some friends this year, and choir would probably mean even more people calling to make plans.

Maybe Trout was busy with school too. Maybe she'd call tonight or tomorrow. Maybe there'd be a letter in the mail soon.

CHAPTER EIGHTEEN

Dear Staggerlee,

It's been a long time, and I hope this letter finds you and yours well. I let the months slip past me without writing or returning your calls, and this morning I climbed out of bed and saw the snow coming down hard and it dawned on me slowly that it was almost February and that four months have passed without us speaking. And I knew then I needed to sit down and write this. I think about Sweet Gum all the time, and when I close my eyes now, I start remembering that line of trees along the water and imagining them heavy with snow.

The letter arrived on a cold day in January, after months and months of silence. Staggerlee read it quickly the first time, sitting cross-legged on her bed, her heart beating hard against her chest.

In my botany class I learned that sweet gum trees are modern-day balm in Gilead. Remember the song Grandma and Grandpa used to sing about the balm in Gilead soothing the wounded soul? When I learned that about sweet gum I started thinking that's why your daddy went back there—maybe because to him the place had some kind of healing feel about it. I don't know. I have study hall fifth period, and sometimes I just sit there thinking. My mind starts wrapping itself around all these crazy ideas.

Staggerlee read, remembering Ida Mae's letter— how it had arrived the same way, a surprise in April. She stared at the words, seeing Ida Mae in Trout.

It's hard to sit in that study hall and not think about you. And I've tried. I sit there with my book propped in front of me and the words start blurring and becoming you standing at the river smiling or you and Creek running fast ahead of me yelling, "C'mon, Trout."

With the snow on the ground, Sweet Gum and last summer seem ancient somehow, dreamy—like it all happened to someone who wasn't me. In two months it'll be a year since Hallique died, but it still seems like last week or yesterday. And some mornings it feels like it happened an hour ago. Me and Ida Mae—I guess we're something like friends now, and maybe it's because of Matthew. I guess that's the hardest part of this letter—the part I haven't been able to write or call you to say. I don't know what I thought you'd do or say or think. Me and Matthew started dating back in September. Every time me and you talked back then, a part of me wanted to tell you that I had met a boy I liked. I wanted to tell you about the parties we go to and how it feels to walk down the street and hold his hand. I wanted to tell you about his smile—how when he looks at me, it seems the world just stops moving. But I didn't know how. Every time we talked, we talked about last summer and we talked about that early morning in your bedroom when you told me about Hazel. I couldn't tell you then, Staggerlee. I didn't know how to. And if I couldn't tell you that, then what could I tell you? It was like you had become Rachel and Rachel had become you. Suddenly I could tell Rachel all about my feelings and I had to keep them hidden from you. Some days I wonder if I'm always going to be hiding something from somebody . . . I hope not. And I figure it's best to start by not hiding from you anymore.

Ida Mae likes Matthew—he eats dinner at our house just about every night and Ida Mae says he has the best table manners of any boy she's ever met. His mama likes me too, I think. She smiles and speaks real sweet to me. Rachel thinks we make a nice couple and sometimes

95

we go out with a few other couples and it's nice when the girls get off alone and we can talk about our boyfriends. It's still strange to write "boyfriend." One day I was sitting in the park alone and I wrote Matthew Loves Tyler in the dirt and it stared back up at me, the words did. They looked bigger than anything, coming up out of the earth like that. And it made me remember that day by the river when I wrote that thing in the dirt. I guess it's strange for you to see me writing "Tyler." Matthew likes it—he thinks it's a pretty name. And the more I write it and look at it, I'm liking it too. I think somewhere inside of me, I'll always be Trout. But I'm Tyler too. The way you used to say about being both black and white—I'm both and all of it.

I'm not writing to say everything's changed. I don't know what I'll wake up feeling tomorrow. But I just needed to write and let you know what I'm feeling today. I just needed to write so I wouldn't have to hide. I want to talk to you—to really talk to you—hear about your life and tell you about mine. I want us to be like we were last summer, close like that, even if we don't have the girl thing in common anymore. And maybe you'll call me tonight and I'll answer and we'll talk for a long, long time.

Love,
Tyler

That afternoon, Staggerlee folded the letter slowly and returned it to its envelope. She sat staring out at the snow, wanting to make sense of it all. She'd have to go back, she knew, if she wanted to remember. "Pull on your boots," she whispered. "Take yourself down to the river."

CHAPTER NINETEEN

Snow fell softly outside her window now. Staggerlee watched it, watched how quietly the flakes moved toward the ground. She swallowed. It had been a month since the letter arrived and still, each time she read it, the words on the page stung.

It seemed like such a short while ago it was summer and she was laying her head against Trout's shoulder. She remembered Trout's voice—the way her mouth moved when she sang. Where was that part of Trout now? Did she still sing? When she was sitting alone with her boyfriend, did she stop to remember that rainy afternoon in the barn?

Staggerlee held the letter in both hands and stared down at it. Downstairs, she could hear her mother moving around the kitchen. She had not told anyone about the letter. And staring at it, she wondered if she ever would. Telling someone would mean starting at the beginning and telling everything. And there was no one she wanted to tell everything to. Maybe one day there would be. Someone she could whisper her life to.

Someone she could take to a party, walk off the edge of the world with. She folded the letter slowly and placed it back inside its envelope. How many times had she read it? Three, four—a hundred?

And each time, the news about Matthew sliced through her. She closed her eyes and tried to wipe out the image of Trout with some boy. Rachel had won, hadn't she? She had found Trout a boyfriend. Staggerlee pressed her head against the pane and stared out at the river. She had thought Trout was stronger than that. She had seemed so sure of herself last summer. But Trout was right—last summer did seem like a long, long time ago.

Staggerlee sighed. Tomorrow was Monday. There was geometry and social science and choir practice to get ready for. There was Lilly in her French class, who giggled, and Abraham in home ec, who swore he made the best pies in all Sweet Gum. She had friends now, people she walked to classes with, people who searched her out in the cafeteria. And some afternoons, if the weather was nice, she biked into town and sat on a milk crate in a circle of Daddy's friends, talking about nothing and laughing about everything.

And Trout? What would she be doing tomorrow? The next day? Next week?

Waiting, Staggerlee thought. They were both waiting. Waiting for this moment, this season, these years to pass. Who would they become? she wondered. Who would they become?

ABOUT THE AUTHOR

Jacqueline Woodson was born in Ohio and grew up in Greenville, South Carolina, and in Brooklyn. She now lives in Brooklyn and in upstate New York. She is the author of several books for young readers, including *The Dear One, From the Notebooks of Melanin Sun,* and a trilogy about best friends Margaret and Maizon: *Last Summer with Maizon, Maizon at Blue Hill,* and *Between Madison and Palmetto.* Her most recent book for Delacorte, *I Hadn't Meant to Tell You This,* was selected as a Coretta Scott King Honor Book in Fiction, a Jane Addams Award Honor Book, an ALA Notable Book, an ALA Best Book for Young Adults, a *Booklist* Editors' Choice, and a *Horn Book* Fanfare. She has also published a novel for adults, *Autobiography of a Family Photo.*

Jacqueline Woodson has been a fellow at the Mac-Dowell Colony and at the Fine Arts Work Center in Provincetown, Massachusetts, and is a recipient of the *Kenyon Review* Award for Literary Excellence in Fiction.